BUDDIES COLLECTION

4 Stories in 1

DISNEP PRESS

LOS ANGELES • NEW YORK

This book belongs to:

_____

First Hardcover Edition, October 2018
1 3 5 7 9 10 8 6 4 2

ISBN 978-1-368-02711-3
FAC-038091-18250

Library of Congress Control Number: 2018937752
Printed in the United States of America

For more Disney Press fun, visit www.disneybooks.com

SUSTAINABLE FORESTRY INITIATIVE   Certified Sourcing
www.sfiprogram.org
SFI-00993
Logo Applies to Text Stock Only

Contents

Do You Want a Hug?

A *Frozen* Story

Written by Kevin Lewis

Illustrated by Olga T. Mosqueda

Hi, there!

I'm Olaf.

And I love,

love,

love
warm
HUGS!

In fact, I am the

KING

of giving them.

So come on.

Let's hug!

I'm waaaiting.

Maybe I should come hug you.

Umph!

Mrfmflm

muffle

mummm

Hmmmmm.
Why didn't that work?

Oh. I get it.

You're playing a game!

If I play a game with you,
will you give me a hug?

Promise?

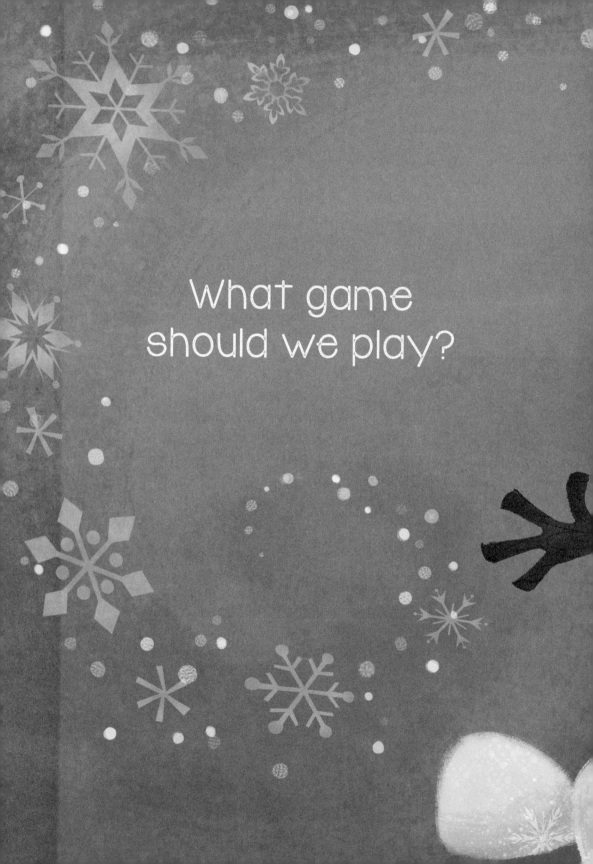

Leap troll?

Ring-around-the-reindeer?

Wheeeeee!

OH! I KNOW!

HIDE-AND-SEEK!

HIDE-AND-SEEK!

HIDE-AND-SEEK!

I'll hide.

You count to ten,

then turn the page.

Done already?

Count again.

BACKWARD this time!

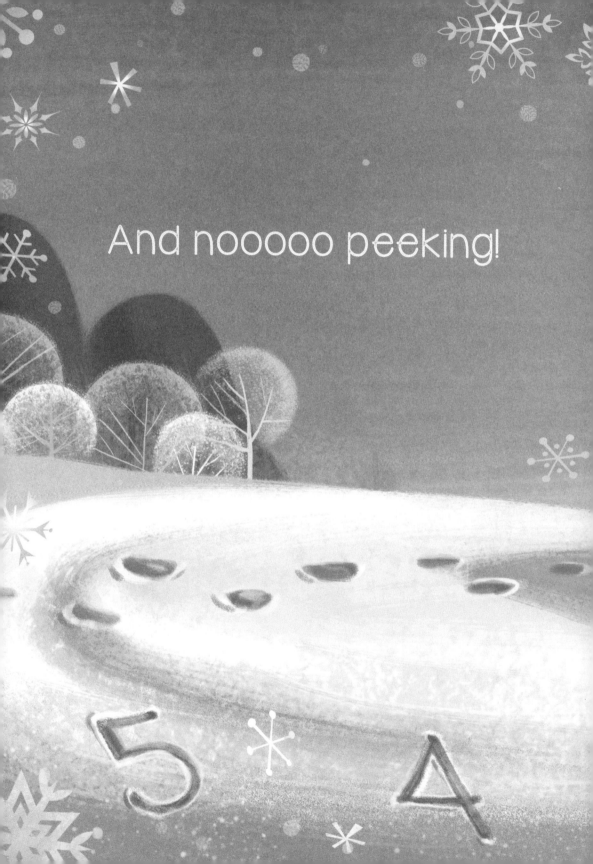

HE-HE-HE

YOU
FOUND
me!

Now how about that HUG!

Dinglehoppers

AND

Thingamabobs

A *Little Mermaid* Story

Written by **Livingstone Crouse**

Illustrated by **Amy Mebberson**

Ahoy, there!

Seagull coming in for a—

-landing.

Oh, hey, kid!

Thought I had this
rock to myself!

Well, as long as you're
here, want to see my
collection?

This . . .

is a
hiffenjugger!

Humans pile these babies
up to see over rocks.

Land ho!

Aha!
The snarfblatt.

Invented to make music
on quiet nights.

Hmmm.

Doesn't work.

Now this one . . .

the pookentick.

Used for spinning in circles!

Whoa!

Hey, kid! Wanna go?

What's that? My hair?
Nice, isn't it?

Batten my hatches, I've been

ruffled!!!

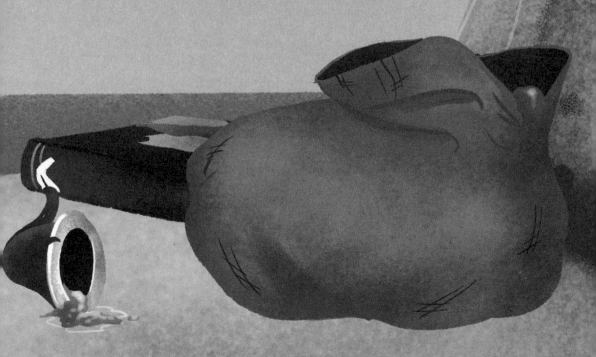

Hang on, kid.
I can fix this.

I just need . . .

No, not that.

I know there's one around
here somewhere.

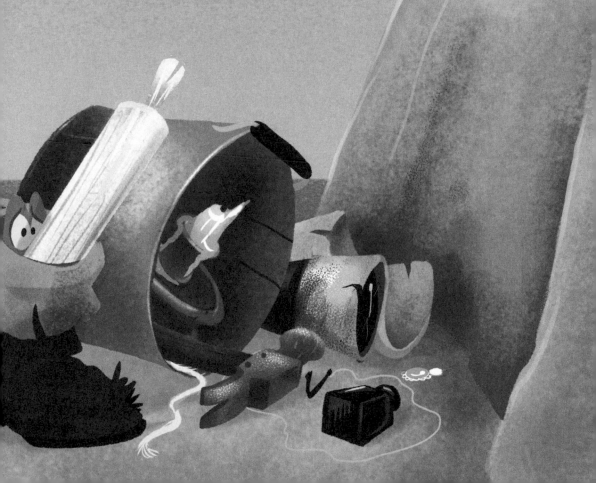

A DINGLEHOPPER!

A twirl here.

A yank there.

And . . .

...voilà!

An aesthetically pleasing configuration of hair!

No good?

Still ruffled?

Never fear.
I've got just the
thing!

This
thingamabob
is perfect for
unruffling feathers,
don'tcha know.

Wrap this here.
Tuck that there.

MAYDAY!

MAYDAY!

Okay, there we go.
A quick tug and . . .

Still

ruffled?

You don't say.

I'm sure this

luggaloop

will work!

Still
ruffled?

This calls for drastic measures.

Time for the

toppenbugle!

UMPH.

Mrflmfl.

Mrflmfl.

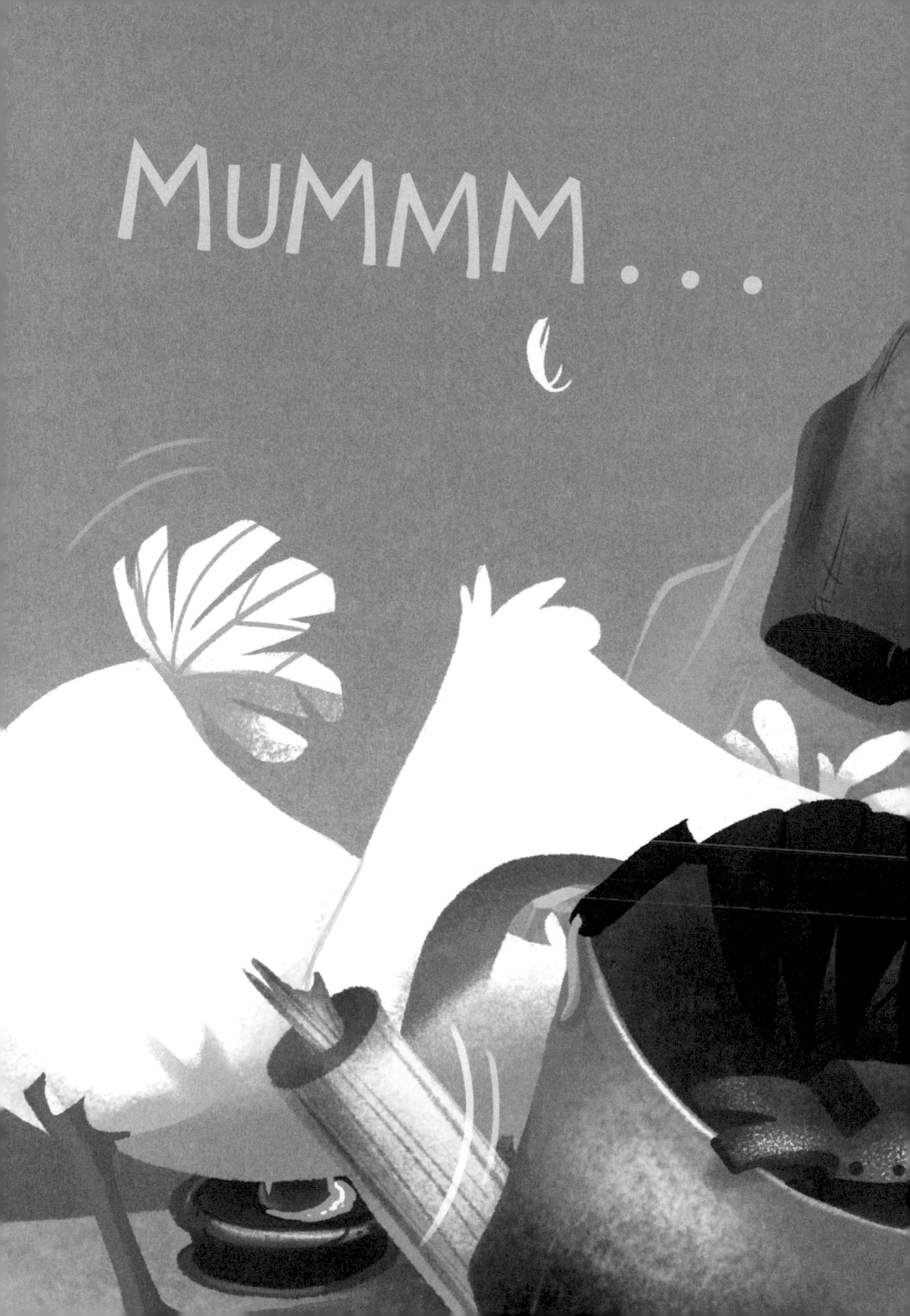
MUMMM...

Whew!

Now that we've got that out of the way, I have a question for you.

Do you happen
to know what

this

doohickey

is?

I Am Not Angry!

An *Inside Out* Story

WRITTEN BY
Marie Eden

ILLUSTRATED BY
Amy Mebberson

Oh, boy.

Here we go again.

I **hate** that helmet!
It pinches our ears!

Seriously.

Doesn't Mom know it gives
us major helmet hair?

Ugh!

But it's so **pretty**!

Don't you like all the
hearts and flowers?

And look.

There are rainbows.
Which come from rain.
I like rainy days.

It's raining?

It's not safe to ride our bike in the rain! We could slip on the hills. And there are cracks in the sidewalk!

Oh, no. No, no, no! We are not going out in the rain!

It's **not** raining, you **nitwit!**

This guy!

He thinks everything is out to get us. Last week it was pigeons. The week before it was Riley's pillow.

Her pillow!

What's scary about a pillow?

What's wrong with *you*?

Angry?

Of course I'm

angry.

Look at what I'm dealing
with here!

What do you mean
I need to **calm down**?

This **is** me being calm!

I'm not yelling.

This is just my voice!

Stop saying that!

How many times do I have to tell you . . .

I think I'm fine, but **someone** keeps telling me to **calm down**.

A good cry usually makes
me feel better. I find
it helps to lie on the floor.

Maybe you should give
that a try.

Is she **serious**?

Fine.

I'll give it a shot.

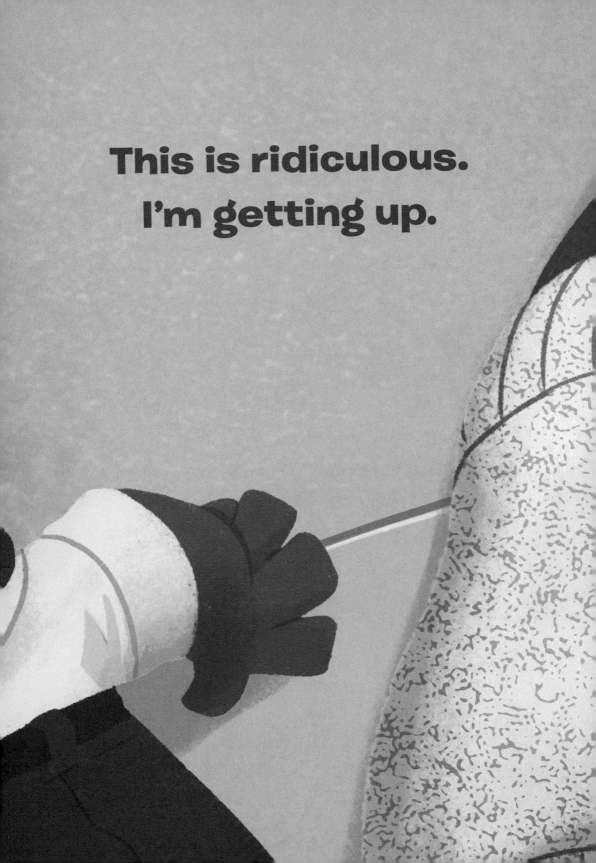

Ugh.

What are you doing lying on the dirty floor?

We're trying to help Anger
calm down. **Shhh.**
Nice, deep breaths . . .

You know that's not going to work, **right**?

Okay, smarty-pants. How do
you calm down?

Actually . . . I have a
memory that always
makes me feel better.
Come on!
I'll show you.

Look at that.

Picture day at school, and
we looked **perfect**!

I bet you feel better now!

Better?

Why would this make me
feel **better**?

Is she **kidding?**

I have a thousand things to do
and **she** has me looking back
at **picture day**?

What are you yelling
about, Anger?
You know, you really
need to **calm down**.

You should do what *I* do
when *I* need to calm down.

Ice-skate with Riley!
Come on!

Ice-skating?
That's her bright idea?

I feel stupid.

Are we **done** with this yet?

Oh, **you** have an idea.
This ought to be **good**.

What do I have to do?

Clench my fists and
pull up my shoulders,
then let out a
loud scream?
That actually sounds like
fun!

Okay, here goes. . . .

Hey, thanks!

I should have known that would work. Yelling always makes me feel better. We should have started with that! But you may want to go check on **Fear**.

Who's
That
Dwarf?

A *Snow White and the Seven Dwarfs* Story

WRITTEN BY
Marie Eden

ILLUSTRATED BY
Amy Mebberson

Ouch!

Why'd you stop?
Now we're going to be late!

What are you looking at?

Well, you're the strangest-looking dwarf I've ever seen.

Where's your **beard?**

Don't be rude!

I think you look just fine
without a beard.

Sure, if you
want to look like
Dopey.

It's not a
bad look!

Where are my manners?

I'm **Happy.**

This is Grumpy.

Don't tell a
complete stranger our
names!

Don't mind him.

We're going to the
diamond mines.

Do you want
to come with us?

Absolutely not.
We are *not* bringing a
stranger to the mines!

What?
We could use the
extra help.

I know!
What you need is a
name!

That way you won't be a stranger anymore!

This should be fun.

You mean funny-*looking*. . . .

Don't mind him.
You look just fine.

Still not much of a
beard....

Okay, let's forget
about the beard.

I can't. It's right there,
not staring me in the face.

Forget. The.
Beard.

I just think dwarfs without beards look **silly**.

Oh, how about
Silly?
We don't have one
of those yet!

Come on,
don't be **shy.**
We already have a
Bashful.

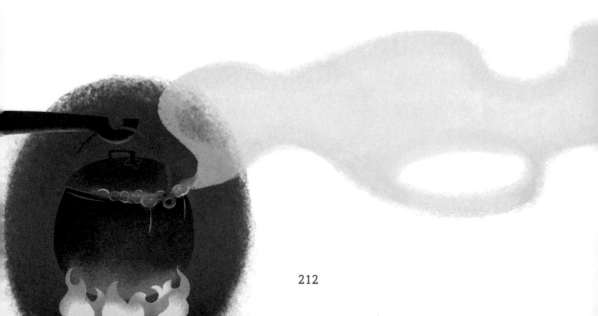

Do you like to eat?

How about Hungry?

Just what we
need, another mouth
to feed.

What are you
complaining about?
We always have
plenty of food!

But what if Sneezy has another **big** kachoo all over our dinner?

Trust me, we won't
run out of food.

We're getting off topic.

The new dwarf
still needs a name!

We have a Doc,
a Sleepy, a Dopey,
a Happy, a Bashful,
a Grumpy, and
a Sneezy.

This is hard!

WAIT! What do you
mean you **already**
have a name?

Have you had a name
all along?

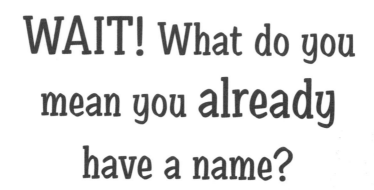

Sheesh.

You could have told us!

Well, this has been a
huge waste of time!

Don't mind him.

That's just how
Grumpy says hi
to new friends.

How about I just call
you friend?